Jack And The Beanstalk

Illustrated By
Craig Berman
Retold From The
Old English Tale

The Unicorn Publishing House, Inc.
New Jersey

Jack And The Beanstalk

Once upon a time there was a poor widow who lived in a little cottage with her son, Jack. The winter before had been hard, and by spring the two had scarely a mouthful of food to eat. The poor woman was ill and couldn't work, and Jack was as yet too young to help.

So one morning she woke her son, and said: "Jack, you must take the cow to market and sell her, for we have no money. I would do it myself, but I am just too weak."

Jack did as his mother asked, and set off for town with their only cow. But it wasn't long before he met up with a strange-looking fellow, who said: "Tell me, young man, would you be interested in selling that fine cow? I am prepared to make you a handsome offer, eh."

The man convinced Jack to sell him the cow for five little beans, which he promised were *really* magic beans. He said they would bring Jack the greatest of luck.

When Jack returned home his poor mother couldn't believe her eyes. "Oh, Jack, what have you done!" she cried. "We shall surely starve now!" And she wept bitterly. Jack felt very ashamed.

Still, at daybreak Jack arose and went out into the garden. There he dug a little hole with a stick, and dropped the five beans in, covering them with a bit of soil. "I know they're probably just plain old beans," thought Jack; "but I just have to do something."

That night they had a little dinner, and then both went sadly off to bed.

When Jack awoke the next morning, he looked out his window, and to his amazement the beans had sprouted! And how they *sprouted!* The stalks twined and twisted up and up and up! Up above the cottage, up above the highest hill, up even to the clouds, where they disappeared from sight.

The stalks were so tightly twisted that they looked like one big stalk, and formed the shape of a ladder. Jack was certain that something wonderful must be at the top of the Beanstalk.

"I wonder where it ends," he thought to himself. "It would be quite easy to climb, I should think." Then with one glance back at the cottage, he grabbed onto the Beanstalk and began to climb.

Jack went up and *up* the Beanstalk until everything below—the cottage, the village, and even the tall church tower—looked quite small, and still he had not reached the top.

After climbing higher still, Jack finally reached the top of the Beanstalk. The young boy stood amazed, finding himself in a beautiful country among the clouds.

Jack looked out upon rich woodlands and beautiful meadows. A crystal stream ran through the pastures, and beyond it there stood a fine, strong castle.

While Jack stood looking at the castle, a strange-looking woman came out of the woods, and walked towards him. Jack made a handsome bow, and asked, "Madam, do you live in that fine home?"

"Oh, heavens no," laughed the old woman, "but I can tell you who does. Once upon a time there was a noble knight, who lived in this castle, which borders on Fairyland. He had great riches, and a beautiful wife and child. But a Giant heard of the riches, and came one night and killed the knight. Luckily, his wife and child were away at the time, which spared them from harm. Word of her husband's death came to her the next day. She took the baby and fled to the land below. There she lives in poverty, raising her son, while the Giant enjoys their riches and the comfort of their castle. Do you know who that woman *is?*"

"Why no, madam, I do not," replied Jack.

"That poor woman is *your* mother, Jack," she said, "and the castle and the riches within are *yours!*"

Jack let out a cry of surprise. "My poor father!" Jack said; "my poor mother! What *must* I do?"

"You must win back the riches and the castle for your mother. It will not be easy to defeat the giant, but defeat him you must." And then she disappeared into thin air, and Jack knew she was a fairy.

Jack wasted no time, and went straightaway to the castle. There he boldly knocked at the door. The door was opened by a frightful-looking Giantess, with one great eye in the middle of her forehead.

As soon as Jack saw her he turned to run away, but she caught him, and lifted him up to have a better look at her little prisoner.

"Ho, ho!" she laughed. "You didn't expect to see the likes of *me*, did you? No, no, I shan't let you go. I will keep you as my little pet, I should think."

The Giantess took Jack into the castle. "I am so weary of my life," she said. "I am so overworked having to care for my ungrateful brother. You shall amuse me and help me with my work. But when my brother is around you must stay hidden, or else he will eat you! And my, what a dainty morsel you would be, my little pet!" Suddenly, thunderous sounds echoed down the hall. The floor and walls began to shake. The Giant was home.

> **Fee, fie, fo, fum,**
> **I smell the blood of an Englishman.**
> **Let him be alive or let him be dead,**
> **I'll grind his bones to make my bread.**

"Oh, don't be silly!" the Giantess said. "You smell the elephant steak I cooked for you. Now stop all this fee, fi, foing about, and sit down to your supper before it gets cold." Spying the steak, the Giant sat down at once and began to feast. When he was through he placed a hen on the table, saying, "Lay me *a* golden egg—no *three* golden eggs." Jack watched as the hen laid three beautiful gold eggs.

Jack knew the Giant had stolen the hen from his father, and he was determined to steal her back. By-and-by the Giant put the hen down on the floor, and soon after went fast asleep, snoring so loudly that it sounded like thunder.

When the Giantess too had gone to bed, Jack stole softly across the room. He picked up the hen and made straightaway for the Beanstalk. He climbed down the Beanstalk just as fast as he could, and by morning's light he reached the cottage.

Jack gave his mother the hen and told her of the fairy, and of his adventures with the Giants. And although the hen would certainly lay enough golden eggs to make them rich, Jack wanted *all* that the Giant *had* stolen from his father. So that evening, he returned back up the Beanstalk.

"*There* you are, my pet," said the Giantess. "Where have you been, you rascal? My brother woke this morning to find his hen was stolen. Now you wouldn't have had anything to do with that, *would* you?" The Giantess laughed, and Jack thought she seemed pleased. Then the Giant came home.

Fee, fie, fo, fum,
I smell the blood of an Englishman.
Let him be alive or let him be dead,
I'll grind his bones to make my bread.

Jack stayed hidden as the Giantess said, "Nonsense! All you smell is this roasted ox I have prepared for your supper. Now sit down and eat." The Giant practically inhaled the huge ox, and when he was done, he pulled out a large sack of gold coins, and began counting. He liked to rub and clink the gold pieces together in his hands, but by-and-by he fell into a deep sleep.

When Jack was sure it was safe, he slipped across the table and gathered the gold pieces up in the bag. Then he was off! back down the Beanstalk.

It was hard work, carrying the heavy money bag down, but Jack managed, and in time he returned to the cottage.

"Here, Mother, I have brought *you* the gold that my father lost."

"Oh, Jack! You are a good boy, but I don't want you to risk your sweet life in the Giant's castle," his mother begged.

"It was *my* father's castle. It is *our* castle," Jack said; and by sunset he had once again made the climb up the Beanstalk.

Again, the Giantess took him in and hid him. "My brother woke to find his bag of gold missing. You are a clever one, you are. But pray you don't get caught, or you shall find *yourself* on my brother's dinner menu." At that moment, the Giant returned.

Fee, fie, fo, fum,
I smell the blood of an Englishman.
Let him be alive or let him be dead,
I'll grind his bones to make my bread.

"You stupid old Giant," she said; "you only smell a nice sheep, which I have grilled for your dinner." And the Giant sat down as a whole sheep was brought for his supper. When he had eaten it all up, he said, "Bring me *my* harp, and I will have a little music before bed." The harp was beautiful, with strings of gold and a frame of diamonds and rubies. The harp sang upon command, and the music was so soft and so sweet that it wasn't long before the Giant fell fast asleep.

Jack ran across the table and grabbed the harp right from under the sleeping Giant's nose. But the harp was really a fairy, and she didn't know Jack was her rightful owner. "Master! Master! Help!" she cried. And the Giant *woke* up.

With a tremendous roar the Giant sprang for the door. But Jack was very nimble. He fled like lightning with the harp. Still the Giant came on so fast that he was ready to grab up poor Jack when they reached the Beanstalk.

Jack jumped onto the Beanstalk and began climbing down. The Giant would have easily caught him then, except for one thing—the Giant was scared of heights. He stopped, and shook a little, as he looked down to the earth far below. This gave Jack time to climb down the stalk, and cry, "Mother, quick! *Bring me the axe!*" For Jack could see that the Giant had regained his nerve, and was coming down the Beanstalk at a furious pace.

There wasn't a second to lose, so Jack took the axe in hand and began hacking away. Jack cut the stem clean through, and in the next moment, the Beanstalk and the Giant came crashing down.

The Giant fell with a loud *thump*, and was dead. The very earth shook from the fall, and people from the nearby village came running to see the once mighty, but now fallen, Giant.

Jack took his mother by the hand, and said, "It will be alright now, Mother; you won't have to worry anymore."

At that moment, the fairy appeared, and smiled at Jack, saying, "You have done well, my young friend. Come, let me take you and your mother back to your rightful home." And she whisked them up through the air to the land among the clouds.

Jack and his mother stood at the castle door and waved good-bye to the Giantess. This was their home now; and in truth, the Giantess had never been happier. She had a whole wide world to see—and beyond.

"Good-bye, my pet, good-bye!" she called back. "I won't forget to send you a postcard! Good-bye!" And the Giantess was off down the road, and on to a new life.

Printing History 15 14 13 12 11 10 9 8 7 6 5 4 3 2 1